Carlotta and Ed
All Year Long

By Sharon Fear
Illustrated by Dominic Catalano

Carlotta and Ed: All Year Long

By Sharon Fear
Illustrated by Dominic Catalano

Wright Group/McGraw-Hill
19201 120th Avenue NE
Bothell, WA 98011
www.WrightGroup.com

Printed in China through Colorcraft Ltd, Hong Kong

10 9 8 7 6 5 4 3

ISBN: 0-322-04508-8
ISBN: 0-322-04604-1 (6-pack)

Contents

CHAPTER 1

Spring Cleaning

It was spring, time to clean house.
Carlotta went to get her broom.
She opened the closet and *wham!*
Out tumbled piles of junk.
There were her old cowboy hat
and her big, red sunglasses.
There was her feather boa!
And her lovely hula-dancer lamp!

"I can't keep all this stuff,"
Carlotta said.
"There just isn't room."
She thought and thought.
"I know! I'll have a garage sale!"

The next day, Ed went to
Carlotta's house.

"What are you doing?" asked Ed.

"I'm having a garage sale,"
Carlotta said with a frown.

"What's wrong?" asked Ed.

"I love these things—my cowboy
hat, my red sunglasses, my
feather boa, and my lovely hula
lamp," said Carlotta.
"But I can't keep them.
I don't have room!"

"Hmmm," said Ed.

He picked up the cowboy hat, the red sunglasses, the feather boa, and the lovely hula lamp.

He gave Carlotta a handful of coins.

"You can borrow them any time."
said Ed.

Carlotta smiled.
"Thanks, Ed!" she said.

"And now I have enough money
to buy something new!
I know just the thing!"

CHAPTER 2

Summer Splash

Carlotta filled her backyard pool.
Ed waved to her. She waved back.

"Come over for a splash!"
she said.

Carlotta put on her new swimsuit
and new sun hat. She made little
sandwiches and a pitcher of
lemonade. She went to sit
by the pool.

came over in his scuba gear.
He jumped in with a big splash!
Carlotta was drenched.
Her sandwiches were soggy.
Her lemonade was full
of pool water.

"Ed!" she cried.
"Do you HAVE to do that?"

"I don't have to," he said, "but it's fun."

"Well, next time, mind your manners!" said Carlotta.

"You're right," he said. "I'm sorry."

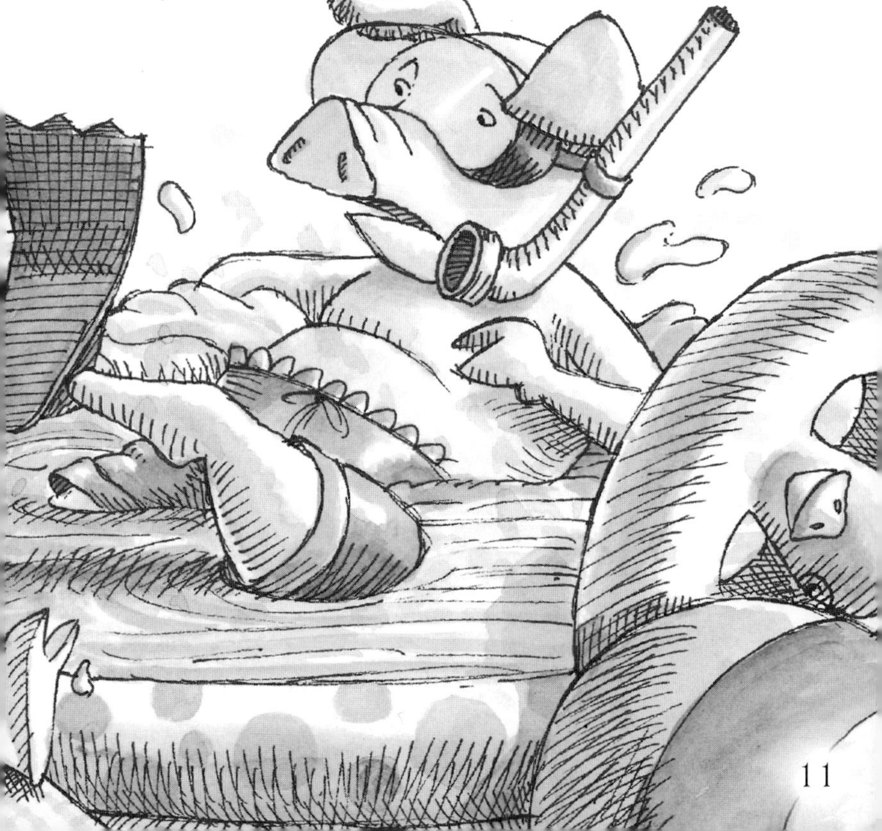

The next day, Ed decided
to mind his manners.
He sat quietly and dangled
his toes in the water.

Carlotta came out with her
big beach ball.
She jumped in with a big splash!
Ed was drenched.

"You're right!" yelled Carlotta.
"It is fun!"

“I told you!” said Ed.
He jumped in, too,
and they had a good splash
together.

CHAPTER 3

Falling Leaves

Ed and Carlotta sat on Carlotta's
porch looking at her maple tree.
The leaves had turned red,
but not one leaf had fallen.

"Those leaves are ready to fall,"
said Ed.

"No they're not," said Carlotta.

"I'm sure they will start falling today," said Ed.

"How sure?" asked Carlotta.

"If they don't fall today," said Ed, "I'll ...I'll ..."

"Bake me cookies!" said Carlotta.

"It's a deal," said Ed.

Carlotta woke early
from her afternoon nap.
She looked out the window.
The leaves were falling fast.
And there was something else!

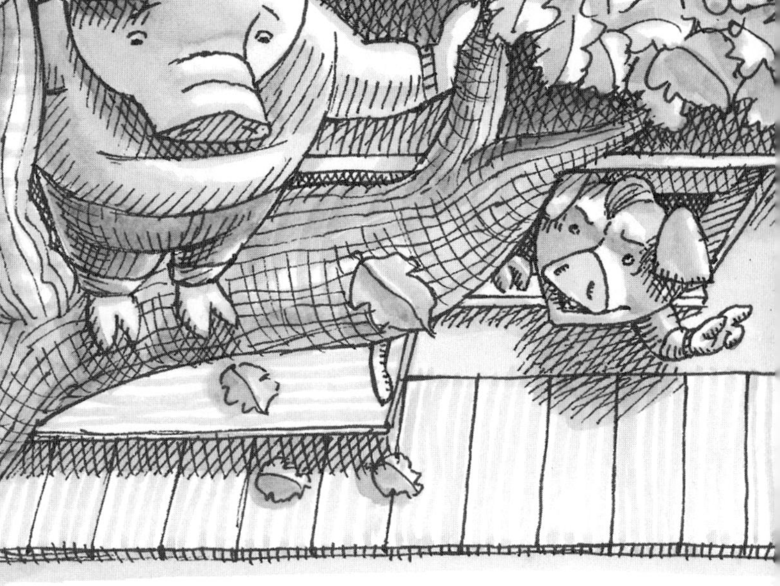

Ed was up there, jumping up and down on the branches.

"I thought you were napping," said Ed.

"Ed, how could you!" said Carlotta.

"I'm so ashamed," said Ed. "But I just couldn't lose. I can't bake!"

"Why didn't you say so, silly!" she said.

Carlotta still made Ed bake cookies. But she helped...a lot.

CHAPTER 4

The Snowman

Carlotta had entered the
Best Snowman Contest.
She really, really, really, really
wanted to win.

But she was worried. Her
snowman wasn't quite right.

Something was missing.

She tried a different scarf.

No.

She tried a cane.

No.

She gave it three eyes.

No, no, no!

Ed brought her a hot drink.

"What do you think?" Carlotta asked.

"Hmmm," said Ed.

"It's terrible, isn't it?" she asked.

"Hmmm," said Ed.

"I give up!" she cried. She stomped into her house and slammed the door.

Later, Carlotta heard a knock.
It was Ed.

"Come out, Carlotta," he said.

But Carlotta was pouting.
"No," she said.

"Don't you want to know who won the contest?" he asked.

"No," she said.

"Won't you PLEASE come out?" he asked.

"Fine," she said.

Ed had been busy.

Carlotta's snowman had on her
old cowboy hat, her red
sunglasses, and her feather boa.
It seemed to be reading by the
light of her old hula-dancer lamp.

"Look, Carlotta," Ed said,
pointing to the ribbon.
"You're a winner."

Carlotta smiled.
"Only because I have a friend
like you."